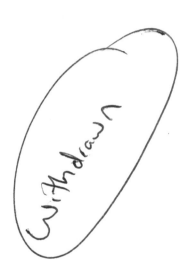

Dora's Sleepover

by Lara Bergen
illustrated by Victoria Miller

Ready-to-Read

Simon Spotlight/Nick Jr.

New York   London   Toronto   Sydney

Based on the TV series *Dora the Explorer*® as seen on Nick Jr.®

SIMON SPOTLIGHT
An imprint of Simon & Schuster Children's Publishing Division
1230 Avenue of the Americas, New York, New York 10020
Manufactured in the United States of America
10 9
Library of Congress Cataloging-in-Publication Data
Bergen, Lara.
Dora's sleepover / by Lara Bergen ; illustrated by Victoria Miller. — 1st ed.
p. cm. — (Ready-to-read) (Dora the explorer)
"Based on the TV series Dora the Explorer as seen on Nick Jr."—T.p. verso.
ISBN-13: 978-1-4169-1508-9
ISBN-10: 1-4169-1508-7
I. Miller, Victoria (Victoria H.) II. Dora the explorer (Television program). III. Title. IV. Series.
V. Series: Dora the explorer
PZ7.B44985Dor 2006
2006014520
0810 LAK

Hi! I am 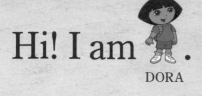.

It is a big night!

I am having a sleepover

with my best friend, ,

BOOTS

at his !

TREE HOUSE

First I need to pack  .

BACKPACK

Do you see what I should

pack?

I will take my ,
PAJAMAS

my , my ,
FLASHLIGHT   SLEEPING BAG

and my of stories.
BOOK   PIRATE

BOOTS loves PIRATE stories!

MAMI has made some **COOKIES**

for **BOOTS** and me. Yum! **MAMI** puts the **COOKIES**

in a **BASKET**.

Do **you** like ?
COOKIES

Thank you, .
MAMI

Good-bye!

How do we get
to 's 🌳?
BOOTS   TREE HOUSE

🗺️ can show us
MAP

the way.

We go through the ,

TUNNEL

then through the ,

JUNGLE

and that's how we get to

's .

BOOTS   TREE HOUSE

We made it to the .
TUNNEL

But the  is **so** dark!
TUNNEL

Is there something

in my that will

BACKPACK

help us see in the dark?

Yeah! A 🔦 !

FLASHLIGHT

We made it through the .

TUNNEL

Now we need to go

through the .

JUNGLE

Uh-oh! Do you see

someone behind that ?

TREE

It is !
SWIPER

 wants to swipe our
SWIPER

 of .
BASKET   COOKIES

Say " , no swiping!"
SWIPER

We stopped .

SWIPER

And there is 's !

BOOTS   TREE HOUSE

We can climb the
LADDER

to get to 's .
BOOTS   TREE HOUSE

Hi,  ! I am ready

BOOTS

for our sleepover!

I have my ,
PAJAMAS

my , my ,
FLASHLIGHT   SLEEPING BAG

my  of  stories,
BOOK   PIRATE

and a  of
BASKET   COOKIES

from  !
MAMI

It is time to put on our .

PAJAMAS

Then we can turn on our

 and eat the .

FLASHLIGHTS   COOKIES

Yum!

I can read my  BOOK

of PIRATE stories

to BOOTS too.

Look at the 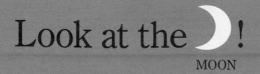! MOON

The is so big and bright. MOON

 yawns.
BOOTS

 is sleepy.
BOOTS

I am sleepy too.

We get into our .

SLEEPING BAGS

Good night, 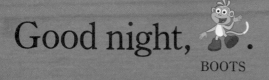.
BOOTS

And good night

to you, too!